For Denise and Klaus

First published in Great Britain in 1994 by Andersen
Press Ltd., 20 Vauxhall Bridge Road, London SW1V
2SA. Published in Australia by Random House
Australia Pty., 20 Alfred Street, Milsons Point, Sydney,
NSW 2061. All rights reserved. Colour separated in
Switzerland by Photolitho AG, Offsetreproduktionen,
Gossau, Zürich. Printed and bound in Italy by
Grafiche AZ, Verona.

ISBN 0 86264 540 9

Suddenly!

Words and Pictures by
Colin McNaughton

A

Andersen Press
London

Preston was walking home
from school one day when
suddenly!

Preston remembered
his mum had asked
him to go to the shops.

Preston was doing
the shopping when

suddenly!

He dashed out of the shop! (He remembered he had left the shopping money in his school desk.)

Preston collected the
money from his desk
and was coming out
of the school when

suddenly!

Preston decided to use
the back door.

On his way back to the shop
Preston stopped at the park
to have a little play when

suddenly!

Billy the bully
shoved past him
and went down the slide!

Preston climbed down
from the slide and went
to do the shopping.
He was just coming out
of the shop when

suddenly!

Mr Plimp the shopkeeper
called Preston back to
say he had forgotten
his change.

At last Preston arrived
home. " Mum," he said.
"I've had the strangest
feeling that someone
has been following me."
Suddenly!

Preston's Mum turned around and gave him an enormous

cuddle!

nee-naa-nee-naa-nee-naa-nee-na

WoLF HOSPiTAL →